ISBN 0 361 09063 3 Hbk

First published in Great Britain by The Macdonald Group 1991
Orbit House, 1 New Fetter Lane, London, EC4A 1AR

A member of Maxwell Macmillan Pergamon Publishing Corporation

Printed and bound in Great Britain by BPCC Hazell Books, Paulton and Aylesbury

CIP data see page 61

All Noddy books are available at your bookshop or
newsagent, or can be ordered from the following address:
Noddy Enterprises, Cash Sales Department, P.O. Box 11,
Falmouth, Cornwall, TR10 9EN.

For all orders (U.K., Overseas, Eire or B.F.P.O.) please send
cheque or postal order (no currency), and allow 80p for
postage and packing for the first book plus 20p for the
second book and 20p for each additional book ordered
up to a maximum charge of £2.00.

NODDY'S ANNUAL 1992

Enid Blyton

Macdonald

Noddy and the Wooden Horse

Now once when Noddy was driving along a country road his car suddenly made a peculiar noise, and then stopped.

"Good gracious! What's wrong with you?" said Noddy, in alarm, and he got out to see. "Your wheels haven't got a puncture, you have plenty of petrol. Then WHY don't you go?"

"Parp-parp," said the car, dolefully, and gave a little rattle.

"I'll have to take you to the garage and get you mended," said Noddy. "Something has gone wrong. But dear me, I'll have to push you all the way because this is a very lonely place and there's nobody to help me."

So he began to push and push, and how he panted and puffed. "I sound like an engine going up a hill!" said Noddy. "Oh dear, I shall never get you to the garage by myself!"

He pushed the car around a corner of the lane, and then he suddenly heard a noise. "Hrrrrrumph! Help! Hrrrrrumph!"

"Now what can *that* be?" said Noddy, and he stood and listened.

"Nay-hay-hay-hay-hay! Hrrrrrumph! Help!"

"Why — it's a horse in trouble!" said Noddy, and he squeezed through the hedge to find it. Sure enough, in the field beyond was a small horse, neighing and snorting loudly.

"What's the matter?" called Noddy.

"I walked into this muddy place," said the horse, "and look — my front legs have sunk down into the mud and I can't get them out!"

Noddy ran to him. "I'll pull you out!" he said. "Which part of you shall I pull?"

"My tail," said the horse. "It's a very strong tail. Hold hard — pull. PULL! Pull HARDER. I'm coming. I'm coming!"

Noddy pulled hard at the wooden horse's tail, and, quite suddenly, the horse's front legs came out of the mud, and the horse sat down heavily on Noddy.

"Oooh, don't!" said Noddy. "I'm squashed flat. Get up, wooden horse. Don't sit on me."

"Sorry," said the horse, and got up. "You really are very kind. It was lucky for me that you

came by just then in your little car."

"Yes, it was," said Noddy. "But I wasn't *in* my car. Something's gone wrong with it, and I've got to push it all the way into Toy Town. Goodness, I shall be tired!"

"You needn't be," said the wooden horse. "I am quite used to pulling carts. I could pull your car for you if you like, all the way to the garage! I'd be glad to do you a good turn, little Noddy."

"Oh *thank* you!" said Noddy. "How lucky I am! Come along — I'll get my ropes and tie the car to you. What fun!"

And off they went — Noddy sitting in his car, steering it carefully, and the little wooden horse walking in front and pulling it well. How everyone stared!

"Aren't I lucky?" called little Noddy. "My car broke down — and I found a little wooden horse to pull it!"

You *were* lucky, Noddy — but, you see, you were kind too, and kind people are *always* lucky!

Spot the Twins

Look at all these dolls in their pretty, spotted frocks. They all look very alike, don't they! Can you help little Noddy spot the twin dolls?

Big-Ears and the Clockwork Clown

One morning when Big-Ears was pegging up all his washing on the line outside his little Toadstool House, a clockwork clown came clicking up. "Hallo, Big-Ears," he said. "What about asking me in for cocoa and biscuits?"

"Certainly not," said Big-Ears. "I know you — you're Jerky the greedy little clown — and you're always wanting food. You must go away!"

He went indoors, and Jerky made a face at his back. "Horrid old Big-Ears!" he said. And what do you think he did then?

He unpegged all the clothes from the line and let them fly away in the wind. What a thing to do!

Big-Ears came rushing out — and caught the naughty little clown. He gave him such a telling-off!

"I'll pay you back for that!" wept Jerky, and ran off. But he didn't go far. He hid nearby in Big-Ears' woodshed.

In the shed he saw a pot of glue and a brush. And dear me, just outside was Big-Ears' bicycle.

And look at what that naughty little clown did! He painted glue on the seat of the bicycle.

And he painted glue on the handles too! Then away he went clickity-click, laughing all over his face!

Well, that afternoon Big-Ears got on his bicycle to ride down to little Noddy's house for tea.

"Dear me — how sticky my bicycle handles feel," he said. "I must wipe them when I get to Noddy's."

He rode all the way through the wood, and into Toy Town, and at last came to House-For-One.

But when he tried to get off his bicycle, he couldn't! He was stuck to the seat. Whatever was the matter?

And then poor Big-Ears found that he couldn't take his hands from the bicycle handles — they were stuck too! He yelled for Noddy. "Noddy! Noddy — quick — I'm stuck!" Noddy came running out in surprise when he heard Big-Ears.

"I'll help you," he said. But no matter how hard he tugged, he couldn't get Big-Ears off the seat.

"I'm *glued* on!" cried Big-Ears, in a great rage. "Noddy, lend me your pyjamas. My trousers are stuck fast!"

So Noddy had to lend Big-Ears his pyjama trousers, and poor Big-Ears left his trousers stuck to the bicycle seat.

He managed to drag his hands away, and then he went into Noddy's house to wash the glue off with hot water.

"You do look funny in my pyjamas," said Noddy. "They're much too small for you! Who could have glued you, Big-Ears?" "I have an idea that Jerky, that naughty little clockwork clown did this," said Big-Ears. "I was cross with him.

"And now I'm *very* cross! I'm going to find him. Get out your car, Noddy, and we'll go and look for him." So they did.

They raced along at top speed to Clockwork-Clown Town — and on Big-Ears' knee was a pot of glue belonging to Noddy!

They soon found out where Jerky lived. Big-Ears banged on his door and he and Noddy walked straight in.

"You get out of my house!" cried Jerky. "You can't walk in like this! What do you want? Let me go!"

Big-Ears handed the pot of glue to Noddy and caught hold of Jerky. "Now Noddy — you paint his key," he said.

"That's it — cover it with glue! Then no one can wind him up! He won't be very pleased about that! But it will certainly teach him a lesson."

Well, Noddy covered the clockwork key with glue — and then Big-Ears stuck a little note on it.

You can see what it said — "Beware — WET GLUE!" The clown *did* feel sorry for himself.

"It serves you right," said Noddy. "You shouldn't have glued my friend Big-Ears to his bicycle! Come on, Big-Ears — we'll go home."

Well of course nobody could wind up Jerky the clown. They all shook their heads and ran away, no matter how much he begged.

His clockwork ran down just as he was going shopping — and there he stopped in the middle of the street.

He stayed there for a whole day until the glue dried, and his brother was able to wind him up once more.

And how glad he was when he could run about again. He went straight to Big-Ears' house and apologised. Then he bought Big-Ears a new pair of trousers. He washed all the things that he'd let blow away and get dirty, and he pegged everything neatly on the line. Big-Ears *was* surprised — and very pleased!

Noddy Goes Riding

Here is Noddy going for a ride on a friendly horse. Why not colour him and Big-Ears with your paints or crayons.

The Seaside is Lovely

One morning, when little Noddy was still fast asleep in bed, somebody rode a bicycle up the path to his little House-For-One.

"Rat-a-tat-a-tat!" Somebody banged so hard on the front door that little Noddy woke up in a hurry and almost fell out of bed in fright.

"Oh dear — who's that knocking? I was fast asleep."

"Rat-a-tat-a-TAT-TAT!"

"Come in, come in, come in," shouted Noddy, beginning to dress in a hurry.

The door burst open and in came Big-Ears, Noddy's friend. He had left his little bicycle outside and he was smiling all over his face.

"Oh, it's you, Big-Ears," said Noddy in surprise. "What do you want to come banging on my door like that for, so early in the morning?"

"I've thought of a plan," said Big-Ears. "I've come to breakfast with you so I can tell you all about it."

"Ooh!" said Noddy. "Do tell me, is it a really BEE-OOO-TIFUL plan, Big-Ears?"

"Yes," said Big-Ears. "I've come to say that we ought to have a holiday today, and we ought to go away to the seaside – at once, now – the sun is shining and it's such a lovely day."

"What's the seaside?" said Noddy, looking excited. "And where is it?"

"Oh Noddy – I keep forgetting how little you know!" said Big-Ears. "The seaside is a lovely place. It's got heaps of yellow sand and a lot of blue water, and you dig in the sand and paddle in the water. You'll love it, Noddy. Will you come? We can go together in your little car."

"Oh *yes* – I'll come anywhere with you, dear Big-Ears, because you are my friend," said Noddy, beaming at him. "Let's have breakfast first. Then we'll leave all the washing-up and go to the seaside straight away. We'll stay all day."

Big-Ears wouldn't go until they had washed-up, made Noddy's bed and put everything very tidy. Then out they went and Noddy slammed his front door behind him. He got out his dear little car and drove it on to the roadway. They packed a picnic and Big-Ears wheeled out his bicycle. "I'll tie it on to the back of the car," he said.

So he did, and off they went together in Noddy's little car, through the streets of Toyland. How excited they were!

Little Noddy began to sing:

"We're off to the sea.
 Big-Ears and me.
 We'll dig in the sand;
 Oh, won't it be grand!
 We'll paddle and play,
 Oh, hip-hip-hooray!"

Noddy drove on and on — and then he suddenly stopped the car and stared. "What's that?" he said, pointing to a big, moving mass of bright blue.

"It's the sea," said Big-Ears. "Isn't it lovely!"

"It's too big," said Noddy. "Much too big. Let's go

and find a dear little sea. This one's too big and it keeps moving. And what are those things that keep rising up to look at us and then falling over with a big splash?"

"They're only waves," said Big-Ears. "Drive on, Noddy. Get nearer."

Noddy drove down on to the yellow sand. He got out and stared at the big, blue sea. He dug his feet into the soft, warm sand.

"Where does the sea end?" he said. "It goes on and on and on and on and . . ."

"Don't bother about where it ends," said Big-Ears. "It *begins* here, anyway. Come on — let's paddle."

"I don't know how to," wailed Noddy. "And I still think the sea's too big. *Please*, Big-Ears, let's go and find a small sea."

"You're silly," said Big-Ears, and took off his shoes and socks. He turned up his trousers and ran down to the sea. He splashed in the little white-edged waves and shouted for joy. "It's lovely, it's lovely! Come and paddle, Noddy, and make a song about it. Oh, do come and feel the water in between your toes!"

All of a sudden Noddy thought he would. He ran to the sea at top speed, and Big-Ears only *just* managed to stop him before he went in with his shoes on. Noddy sat down and took them off.

Then he ran to join Big-Ears, and the two of them paddled up and down, up and down, making splashes as they went.

"This is better than splashing in puddles after

the rain," said Noddy, joyfully. "There's much more water to splash with. Oooh — *that* was a big splash, wasn't it, Big-Ears? Did I wet you?"

"Yes, you did," said Big-Ears. "Look out — there's quite a big wave coming."

Noddy jumped up and down in the wave joyfully, and sang a song at the top of his voice:

"The sea is big,
 The sea is blue,
 It's big enough
 For me and you,
 It's big enough for everybody —
 Come and splash with
 little Noddy!"

Noddy jumped so high that he suddenly fell over — SPLASH!

There he was, lying in the water, looking very surprised and rather frightened.

"Oh, I'm wet! Oh, the sea's cold! Oh, there's a wave running over me! Help, Big-Ears, help!"

Big-Ears helped him up. "You're wet through," he said. "I knew that would happen. I shall take you back home if you do silly things, Noddy."

"Oh no, no, no!" shouted Noddy, beginning to splash about again. "The seaside is lovely, lovely, lovely!"

Noah's Ark

The animals are lost! Can you help Noddy
to show them the way back to Mr and Mrs
Noah and their ark?

Noddy's Ludo Game

Noddy's Ludo Game can be played by 2, 3 or 4 players. You will need a die and 4 counters, each of the same colour, for each player.
Put your 4 counters in the matching coloured squares next to Noddy, Big-Ears, Mr Plod or Mr Noah. Take turns to throw the die. The player who throws the highest number starts the game. Start on the square marked with an arrow and go round the board in the direction of the arrow. When you reach a coloured square that matches your counter you can start to move towards the square marked HOME. Each player throws once each time, but if you throw a 6 you have a second throw. Move your counters forward the number of places shown on the die. If you land on a space that already has a different coloured counter on it you must go back to the beginning. The winner is the player whose 4 counters reach HOME first.

HOME

HOME

HOME

HOME

A Bag of Mixed Spells

One day Miss Fluffy Cat came to ask Noddy to take her to Magic Village in his little car. They set out, and Miss Fluffy Cat told Noddy that she wanted to get herself a new tail there.

Noddy had never been to Magic Village, so he felt quite excited. "Here we are," said Miss Fluffy Cat.

Magic Village was full of little crooked cottages and odd towers and strange little shops.

While Miss Fluffy Cat went to get herself a new tail, Noddy looked in at the shop windows. What strange things he saw!

"I'll buy something to take home!" he thought. "I'll buy a bag of Mixed Spells, and try them. What fun I shall have with them!"

He bought the bag of Mixed Spells, and then Miss Fluffy Cat called him. "I'm ready to go home," she said. She had had a most beautiful new tail put on by magic, and she wore her old tail for a collar. She looked really nice.

They set off home and Noddy told Miss Fluffy Cat about his Mixed Spells. "Be careful, Noddy!" she said.

They got back to Toy Town and Miss Fluffy Cat paid him six pence. Her beautiful new tail waved proudly.

"I think I'll go to tea with Big-Ears and take this bag of Mixed Spells to show him," said Noddy.

Big-Ears was very pleased to see him. "Come in," he said. "What have you got there, little Noddy?"

"A bag of Mixed Spells!" said Noddy, and shook a lot of little coloured boxes on to the table.

Big-Ears picked one up. "Vanishing pill," he read on the lid. He took out a small, round yellow pill.

But it slipped from his fingers to the floor — and in a trice Big-Ears' big black cat had pounced on it.

She swallowed it. BANG! She disappeared at once, and left only a little bit of white smoke!

"Oh! My cat! She's gone!" cried Big-Ears. "You and your silly spells, Noddy — now see what's happened!"

"Well, *you* dropped it!" said Noddy. He went down on his hands and knees, calling, "Puss, Puss, Puss!"

But no cat came, of course. Noddy stood up and took another box from the table. "Perhaps . . ." he began.

But Big-Ears was so upset and angry that he threw the rest of the boxes into the fire!

BANG! POP! BANG! Fizzle-whoosh, fizzle! BANG! Whatever was going on! Noddy ran outside in fright.

And would you believe it, as he stood there, Big-Ears' Toadstool House began to melt.

Yes, it melted just as if it had been made of snow. Noddy called to Big-Ears, "Where are you?"

But nobody answered. The Toadstool House just melted away, and nothing was left but a slushy puddle.

It ran round Noddy's feet, and felt as sticky as treacle. Oh dear, oh dear, what a dreadful thing!

Poor Noddy jumped into his car, crying big tears, and drove off to Miss Fluffy Cat's. She might help him.

"How silly you are to play about with spells!" she said. "Are there any left, little Noddy?"

"No," said Noddy, and then he remembered the one he had picked up from the table. "Just one," he said.

"Ah — this is a Come-Back Spell," said Miss Fluffy Cat. "Go back straight away and throw it on Big-Ears' melted house."

So back Noddy went in his car. He drove at top speed. Soon he was at the spot where the Toadstool House had melted.

He threw the Come-Back Spell into the treacly mess — and hey presto, look what happened!

The big toadstool stalk grew up — then the top — and next the little chimney appeared.

And there was the window — and the door! Noddy ran and opened it — was dear old Big-Ears inside?

Yes, he was, looking most surprised. "Whatever happened?" he said. "Oh, there's my old cat back again!"

"Oh what a good thing I had that one spell left!" said Noddy, hugging Big-Ears. "What a very good thing!

"I'll never buy spells again, Big-Ears. Oh, I'm glad you're back!" And Noddy and the cat did a happy dance.

Count the Apples

Noddy, Big-Ears and Mr Wobbly Man have been picking apples. Can you see who has picked most?

The Day of the Concert

The day of the school concert drew near. What fun it was going to be! Everyone was doing something.

"I'm doing a sailor dance," said the sailor doll.

"We're singing a skittle song," said the skittles. "And then Billy Ball is going to roll on the stage and knock us all down! We're going to yell like anything."

"I'm singing a quacking song," said the toy duck proudly.

"I'm saying a poem about a sweep," said Martha Monkey. "I've got a sweep's brush too. If I don't like your quacking song, Dilly Duck, I'll sweep you away with my brush."

"You won't," said Noddy, who was very fond of the little toy duck. "I'll see you don't! I'll hide your brush!"

"I'm doing a nice growly song," said little Tubby Bear. "I've been practising it at home."

"Oh — so *that's* what you've been doing," said Noddy. "I kept hearing you every night. I thought you must be ill."

"We're doing a fairy dance," said the two pretty fairy dolls.

"I shall clap and clap!" said Noddy, who thought the fairy dolls were just about the prettiest dolls he had ever seen. "And I shall nod my head like anything."

"What are *you* going to do, Noddy?" asked Clara Kitten.

"Nothing," said Noddy, sadly. "Miss Prim says I'm not good enough to sing. And I can't dance well, because my left foot gets in the way of my right one. And I can't say a poem because I keep forgetting what comes next. And I can't quack or growl, although I've tried hard. I can only nod my head."

"You're not very clever," said Martha Monkey. "Not at all clever. Fancy not doing anything at the concert!"

"You won't get a single prize," said the sailor doll, unkindly.

"I can't help it," said Noddy, hanging his head. "I

could sing one of my own songs, but people would think me very vain if I did. And I'm trying not to be, so that I don't get a swollen head, like people who think they're clever."

Well, the day of the concert came at last, and everyone arrived to hear the toys and see them. Mrs Duck came to hear Dilly Duck, Mr and Mrs Monkey came to see Martha Monkey, and Ma Skittle came to hear all the little skittles singing. There was quite a crowd in the schoolroom.

Miss Prim had had a platform put up at one end of the room. Her pupils were longing to begin the concert, and at last it was time. They all came on together and sang the opening song. Noddy too. Big-Ears was there, and he waved to him. Dear old Big-Ears — how nice of him to come, even though Noddy wasn't doing anything by himself at the concert, and wasn't even having a prize!

You would have loved that concert! It was wonderful. Dilly Duck quacked her little song and everyone clapped. Look at her, isn't she sweet?

Martha Monkey was a great success, and swept a
pretend chimney so hard when she said her poem
that she almost swept the piano off the platform.

Little Tubby Bear was clapped so loudly that he
had to come on and do his growling song all over
again. Noddy clapped him till his hands nearly
wore out!

At the end the little clockwork mouse was
supposed to take a bunch of flowers and give them
to Miss Prim with a nice little speech. But just at
the last minute he said he couldn't do it!

"I can't! I can't! I'm too shy! I shall forget what I've got to say! I shall swallow my long whiskers! I shall fall over my tail!" he squealed.

"Well, somebody else must do it," said Martha Monkey. "I can't. I'm no good at that sort of thing. Besides, I don't know the speech that the clockwork mouse was going to make."

Nobody knew it except the clockwork mouse. Oh dear — whatever were they to do?

"Well — I do like Miss Prim so much," said Noddy, at last. "I can't bear her not to have her flowers, and a nice little speech. *I'll* do it — and if I make a muddle of it, well, I just can't help it!"

So Noddy went bravely on to the platform all by himself, with an ENORMOUS bunch of flowers. What was he to say? Oh dear, do think of something, Noddy!

And, will you believe it, a little song came into his head, all about Miss Prim! What a lucky thing. Noddy sang it out at the top of his voice:

> "Hurrah for Miss Prim,
>   She is perfectly sweet,
>   From the hair on her head
>   To the toes on her feet.
>   She teaches us writing,
>   She teaches us sums,
>   And everyone's happy
>   Whenever she comes!

Three cheers for Miss Prim,
Hurrah and hooray,
Our concert is over,
That's all for today!"

And then little Noddy went up to the smiling and
surprised Miss Prim, bowed very low and gave her
the flowers. She really was delighted!

Mrs Tubby's Tea Party

See how well you can paint or crayon this
picture of Mrs Tubby's tea-party.

Noddy Climbs a Tree

"Here I go
In my little car,
Bumpity-bump,
How happy
  we are!"

That was the song little Noddy was singing as he drove through the woods. He had just taken Mrs Monkey to stay with her sister in Monkey Town and now he was coming back at top speed through the trees.

The path was very rough — bumpity-bump went the car and Noddy bounced up and down in the driving seat.

"I feel as if I were riding on a horse!" he said. And then, quite suddenly, the little car stopped.

Noddy was surprised. "What's the matter with you?" he said. "I didn't make you stop. Have you got a puncture in one of your tyres?"

"Parp-parp-parp-parp-PARP!" said the little car, as if it wanted to tell Noddy something important.

Noddy wondered
what it could be
saying. He looked all
round him — and then
he suddenly heard a voice
calling in fright.

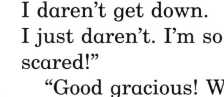

"Oh help, help! Oh, I shall
fall! Oh, help, help, please!"

"Dear me — somebody must be
in trouble," said Noddy, and he got
out of his car at once. He stood and
listened. Where was the shouting coming from?

"It seems to be coming from high up," said Noddy
to himself. "Perhaps it's somebody up in a tree?"

So he went to look — and then, high up in a big tree
he saw something blue. He looked hard, and then he
saw little Connie Kitten in her new blue dress.

"Connie Kitten! What's happened?" he called.

"Oh, is that you, little Noddy?" shouted Connie
Kitten. "Please help me! I've climbed up this tree and
I daren't get down.
I just daren't. I'm so
scared!"

"Good gracious! Why
ever did you climb it
then?" asked Noddy,
climbing up the tree
himself.

"Well, a bird called
something rude after
me and I thought I
would climb up to
its nest and take its

eggs," said
Connie Kitten.

"That wasn't
very nice of you,"
said Noddy. "You
shouldn't take
birds' eggs, you
know that."

"Well, I wish
I hadn't climbed
up now," said Connie
Kitten, beginning to cry.
"I'm frightened. I couldn't
reach the nest, and now that
horrid bird is laughing at me."

"Well, look — put your foot
just *here*," said little Noddy, taking
hold of Connie Kitten's ankle and pulling it gently
down to a lower branch.

But she screamed loudly and clutched the trunk of
the tree tightly. "No, no — I shall fall, I know I shall.
You must carry me down."

"Don't be silly, I can't do that," said Noddy. "I'm not
big enough. Look — just tread *here*, and then . . ."

"No!" squealed Connie Kitten. "I'm afraid of climbing down. Get somebody to come and carry me
down."

"All right," said Noddy and began to climb down.
"I must say that I think you are very, very silly,
Connie Kitten."

When he was halfway down Connie Kitten squealed again. "I'm falling! I feel giddy! I shall fall right down and hurt myself. Come back, Noddy, and hold me."

Noddy climbed back as fast as he could. Connie Kitten had her eyes closed and she certainly looked frightened! Noddy put his arm round her.

"Don't fall. Don't let go. I'm holding you. But how can I get help if I have to stay up here with you and hold you all the time, Connie Kitten?" he said.

"I don't know," said Connie Kitten, clutching at Noddy and almost making him lose his balance. "I know I shall fall! Oh, why ever did I think I could climb a tree, and in my new dress, too!"

Noddy suddenly had a very good idea. He took his scarf and put it round a nearby branch — and he put it round Connie Kitten too! He knotted his nice yellow scarf tightly — and there was Connie Kitten, tied fast to the branch!

"There!" said little Noddy, pleased. "You're quite safe now, Connie Kitten. Even if you fall, the scarf will hold you up. Don't be afraid any more. I'm going to climb down and get Big-Ears, my friend, to come and rescue you. He's very strong."

"I do think you're clever, little Noddy!" said Connie Kitten. "I'm not frightened now."

Noddy climbed down the tree again and ran to his

car. "I'll soon come back with Big-Ears!" he said, and away he went to Big-Ears' Toadstool House.

Big-Ears was at home, which was lucky. "Come at once, Big-Ears!" cried Noddy. "Connie Kitten's up a tree and she can't get down! I've tied her tightly to a branch with my scarf, but she feels very, very giddy."

"Dear me — that Connie Kitten is always getting into some fix or other!" said Big-Ears, and he got into Noddy's car. Off they went. Noddy drove to the big tree and called out loudly, "Connie Kitten! Here we are. Don't worry, Big-Ears is going to

climb up and carry you down."

There was no answer, so Noddy called again and Big-Ears got out of the car. He peered up the tree.

"No wonder there isn't an answer!" he said. "There's nobody there. It must be the wrong tree!"

"It isn't, it isn't!" said Noddy, and he got out to look too. But dear me. Connie Kitten wasn't there!

"Drive your car round and about and shout," said

Big-Ears, rather cross. So Noddy drove round and yelled at the top of his voice. But Connie Kitten didn't answer him.

"It was just a joke she played on you!" said Big-Ears. "She must have climbed down as soon as you had gone, and run home laughing — with your nice yellow scarf!"

"Goodness me — the horrid kitten!" said Noddy, in a rage. "I'm going to go to Connie Kitten's home right now and give her a good telling-off!"

And dear me, off he went in a dreadful temper. Look out, Connie Kitten — here comes a very angry Noddy!

He came to Connie Kitten's house and banged the door — blam, blam, blam! He put a big frown on his face, and his head nodded very fast indeed — nid-niddy-nod-nid-niddy-nod!

The door opened — and there was Connie Kitten, all smiles! "Oh, it's *you*, Noddy! I was just ironing your scarf, all ready to bring back to you, it was so crumpled with knots. My uncle, Mr Whiskers Cat, came by just after you had gone, and he untied me and lifted me down."

"Oh," said Noddy, and his frown flew off his face at once. "I thought perhaps you had been playing a horrid trick on me, Connie Kitten."

"Oh *no*! I just wanted to iron your scarf — and look, I bought you a nice little scarf-pin on my way back," said Connie Kitten, showing him a beautiful scarf-pin. "I was going to call at your house and leave them for you. Oh, Noddy, I *do* think you are clever — nobody else but you would ever have thought of tying me to the tree with a scarf!"

Noddy was very, very pleased. "I was going to be cross with you," he said, "but now I am pleased and I want to buy you an ice-cream. Let's get into my car and we'll go."

"Put your scarf on first," said Connie Kitten, and he put it on and proudly put in his new scarf-pin. Off they went and Noddy sang his little song!

"Here we go in my little car,
    Bumpity-bump, how happy we are!"

Noddy and Mr Tubby set off in Noddy's car to go and see Big-Ears at Toadstool House but they have many stops on the way and it takes them a very long time. Can YOU get there more quickly? Ask an adult for a different colour counter or button for each player and a die in an egg-cup. You then take turns to throw, but you must get a six to start.

Bad Mr Grab

One day, when Noddy was just finishing his breakfast, a knock came at his door. "Who is it?" called Noddy. "Someone come to hire your car," said a voice, "for a long journey!" Noddy went to the door at once.

Outside stood a strange-looking fellow, rather like one of the goblins who lived in the woods.

"I'm Mr Grab," he said. "I want to go to Faraway Town." Noddy went to get his car.

"That's a very, very long way," he said. "Have you enough money to pay for such a long journey?"

Mr Grab opened a bag he was carrying and let Noddy look inside. It was full of gold money!

"My word — you *are* rich!" said Noddy. "Get in, please." Off they went, Mr Grab sitting beside Noddy.

Now, when they came to a very lonely place, Mr Grab ordered Noddy to stop the car. Noddy stopped it in surprise.

"Get out now," said Mr Grab, "because *I* want your car. From now on it's *my* car not yours!"

"It isn't!" cried Noddy, in alarm. "You're a bad goblin, Mr Grab. I believe you stole that money."

But dear me, the naughty goblin gave poor Noddy a big push, and out he fell into the road. Then r-r-r-r-r-r- . . .

Mr Grab started the car again and raced away up the road at sixty miles an hour. What a wicked goblin he was!

Noddy sat and wailed. "Oh dear! What am I to do? I don't know where I am, and my dear little car is stolen!"

Mr Grab and the car were out of sight. Noddy walked along the road, shedding big tears as if he were raining.

Another car came along the road. "Stop!" cried Noddy. The car stopped and a very smart toy dog looked out.

"Please will you chase a thief who has taken my car?" said Noddy. "Jump in," said Mr Dog, and away they went.

But they couldn't see any sign of Mr Grab. Mr Dog set Noddy down further from home than ever!

"It's no good going after that goblin!" he thought sadly. "I'll have to walk all the way home!"

He got a lift on Master Bert Bear's motor-bicycle, but Noddy's hat kept blowing off.

At last Bert Bear angrily told him to get off, and went roaring away by himself.

Then Noddy got a lift in a farmer's hay-cart, but alas, he fell asleep and tumbled out of the cart.

As the old farmer was deaf, he didn't hear Noddy shouting — so there he was all alone again!

He walked and he walked, and at last he came to a little railway station. He waited for the train to come along.

But it was going the wrong way, so Noddy set off walking again, thinking of all the things he would like to do to Mr Grab!

And then what did he hear but a bicycle bell — and round the corner came his dear old friend Big-Ears on his little bicycle!

He *was* surprised to see Noddy and hear his sad tale. "Get on the back of my bicycle and we'll fetch Mr Plod," he said.

So off they went together to find Mr Plod. "Here's the police station," said Noddy. "I'll knock!" Blam-blam. Mr Plod opened the door. "Oh Mr Plod, my car has been stolen, and it must be in Faraway Town by now!" said Noddy.

"No, it isn't," said Mr Plod, with a great big smile on his face. "Look!" And he opened a door inside the police station.

There was Noddy's little car in Mr Plod's sitting room! "I'll tell you how it came here," said Mr Plod, still smiling.

"It wouldn't take that bad Mr Grab to Faraway Town. As soon as it came to a corner, it went the opposite way. And it came back here at top speed, so that Mr Grab didn't dare to get out. And then it ran through my front door.

"It came hooting into my sitting room where I was sitting! I did get a shock! So I seized Mr Grab.

"And now he's locked up in a cell, and I've got all the money he stole!" Noddy *was* surprised.

"You're the cleverest car in the world!" said Noddy, patting it. "Let's go home, Big-Ears, and have a fine tea."

And they drove right out of Mr Plod's big front door, hooting loudly. Good gracious — HOW surprised everyone was!

Big Ears' Toadstool House

You can use your crayons or pens to colour in this picture of Noddy and Big-Ears.

Tom Kitten's Trick

One day Noddy thought he would go fishing and catch a big fish for his dinner.

"Then I will ask Big-Ears and Tessie Bear to have dinner with me, and I shall feel very proud!" said Noddy. "I will go and ask Big-Ears right now."

So he went knocking at Big-Ears' Toadstool House. "Big-Ears — please come to dinner with me today. I am going to catch a big fish."

He asked little Tessie Bear too, and she was very pleased. "I'll come," she said. "And I'll help you cook the dinner."

Well, Noddy
set off with his rod
and line, and soon he came to a big, round pond. "I
shall catch my fish here," he said, and he sat down
on the bank and began to fish.

Soon, along came little Tom Kitten and he
grinned at Noddy. "There are no fish in that pond!"
he said.

"You don't know anything about it!" said Noddy.
"Go away, Tom Kitten. You're always teasing
people."

"Big-Ears is looking for you," said Tom Kitten.
"He's over there."

Noddy put down his rod and ran to find Big-Ears
at once. Naughty Tom Kitten grinned. He knew
that Big-Ears wasn't anywhere near — he just
wanted to play a little trick on Noddy!

Do you know what he did? He had seen an old
boot in the pond, and quickly he waded in and fixed
the boot to the end of Noddy's line! How he laughed!

Noddy came back, very cross! "Big-Ears wasn't
looking for me. He wasn't anywhere to be seen, you

bad kitten."

He picked up his rod — and dear me, he felt
something on the end of the line at once! "A fish! I've
caught a fish!" he cried. "My goodness me, it's a BIG
one!"

Noddy pulled and pulled, trying to bring up the
big fish — and at last up it came. There was the
boot, dangling on the end of his line.

Tom Kitten rolled over and over on the grass and
laughed until he cried. "Ho, ho, ho! *I* put it there!
You thought it was a great big fish! Oh, what a tale.
I'll tell everyone in the village!"

"You're very unkind," said Noddy. "I thought it
was such a big fish — and I was going to cook it for
dinner and I've asked Big-Ears and Tessie Bear to
come, and . . ."

"Ho, ho, ho!" laughed Tom Kitten. I'll go and tell them they'll have fried boot for dinner, with boot-lace sauce!"

"Hallo — what's all this noise about?" a voice suddenly said, and up came big Mr Burly Bear. "Why, little Noddy — I *do* believe you've caught the boot I lost in the pond last winter when I skated on it and the ice broke! I fell in and lost one of my boots — and here it is back again! I shall dry it out and wear it again. Noddy, you really are very, very clever!"

"Am I?" said Noddy, and his head nodded up and down fast because he was very pleased.

"You are," said Mr Burly Bear. "Look, here is a whole pound for catching my boot. You go and buy a fish at the fishmonger's and give a little party."

"Oh, *thank* you!" cried Noddy. "I'll go this very

minute. Ha, ha, Tom Kitten — you played a trick on me, but *you're* the one who looks silly now!"

And off he went to buy a nice big fish for dinner. Then he went back to his little house to cook it, with little Tessie Bear to help him, and Big-Ears to lay the table.

"We're going to have a very nice time," said Noddy. "And all because I caught a boot instead of a great big fish!"